Miss Lilly Is Leaving

Based on the stories by Katharine Holabird
Based on the illustrations by Helen Craig

Grosset & Dunlap

Library of Congress Control Number: 2006024525

ISBN 978-0-448-44473-4   10 9 8 7 6 5 4 3 2 1

Alice stood in the candy aisle at Mrs. Thimble's General Store. The jars were full of colorful candies and crunchy snacks, and Alice was having a terrible time choosing.

Just then she overheard Miss Lilly and Mrs. Thimble chatting at the counter. "Remember to cancel my milk delivery," said Miss Lilly. "And the *Mouseland Gazette*. I shall miss it."

"We shall miss you, too," said Mrs. Thimble. "But it's not every day that you can teach at such a wonderful school!"

Alice sucked in her breath. Where was Miss Lilly going? Was she leaving Chipping Cheddar—and her ballet students—behind?

Angelina was practicing ballet when Alice burst into the bedroom.

"Angelina!" cried Alice. "Miss Lilly is leaving us. I heard it with my own ears!"

Angelina took another twirl across her bedroom floor. "Don't be silly," she said. "Miss Lilly wouldn't leave us!"

But as Angelina neared the window, she heard voices from down below. There, just outside the Mouselings' front gate, stood Miss Lilly and Mrs. Hodgepodge.

"Would you be so kind as to water my flowers?" Miss Lilly was saying. "I know they'll be in such good hands."

"Oh, no," whispered Angelina. Miss Lilly really *was* leaving!

At ballet class that afternoon, Angelina and Alice shared
the terrible news with their friends.

"I saw Miss Lilly in Mrs. Thimble's shop," began Alice.

"She's canceled her milk delivery!" exclaimed Angelina.

"And her newspaper," added Alice.

"And Mrs. Hodgepodge is going to water her flowers!" cried Angelina.

The other mouselings gasped, but before they could ask questions, the studio door creaked open and Miss Lilly stepped into the room.

"Are you ready, my darlinks?" she called to them.

Angelina and the other mouselings tried to focus on dancing, but they couldn't stop worrying about Miss Lilly leaving. Priscilla and Penelope Pinkpaws bumped into each other, and when William tried to lift Angelina into the air, he wobbled and nearly dropped her.

"What has gotten into all of you today?" Miss Lilly gently scolded them. "You've had weeks to learn these steps."

Angelina hung her head and said softly, "Sorry, Miss Lilly. We didn't mean to disappoint you."

Miss Lilly sighed. "I'm sure you didn't," she said. "Now practice, darlinks. Practice those steps!"

When the telephone rang, Miss Lilly stepped into her office. Angelina and Alice glanced at each other anxiously. Should they listen in? Angelina crouched down and pressed her ear to the door.

"Is everything ready for me at the Rodentski Academy?"
Miss Lilly was saying. "I can't wait to teach those magnificent
mouselings! I'll be on the first train tomorrow."

Tomorrow? Angelina couldn't believe that Miss Lilly would
be leaving so soon!

When Miss Lilly returned to the classroom, the mouselings were dancing their very best. Angelina skipped gracefully around William. She was determined to prove to Miss Lilly that she and her friends were just as magnificent as the dancers at the Rodentski Academy.

But later, at home, Angelina felt miserable. Her mother tried to cheer her with cheese muffins, fresh from the oven.

As Angelina bit into a warm muffin, she *did* feel better. Suddenly, she had an idea. "May I take more?" she asked her mother.

A short while later, Angelina stood on Miss Lilly's front step. Angelina took a deep breath and then knocked on the door.

"Hello, Miss Lilly," Angelina said sweetly when her teacher appeared at the door. "I've brought you some of my mother's cheese muffins."

"Why, Angelina—" began Miss Lilly, but before she could say anything more, Priscilla and Penelope Pinkpaws skipped up the steps with a beautiful bouquet of flowers.

"These are for you, the best ballet teacher in the whole world!" said Penelope.

"What have I done to deserve this?" exclaimed Miss Lilly. "You're so thoughtful!"

Alice was the last of Miss Lilly's students to arrive. Poor Alice was in such a hurry that she tripped and spilled her basket of red berries at the bottom of Miss Lilly's steps.

"Oh, dear," said Alice, quickly gathering the berries. "I was picking berries and thought you'd like some, Miss Lilly."

"Why, thank you, my darlinks!" said Miss Lilly. "I'm so touched." She smiled warmly at the mouselings and then said, "But now, I really must get on with my packing."

Back at home, Angelina slumped onto her bed and let the tears fall. Her plan had failed, and Miss Lilly would be gone in the morning. "It's just not fair," Angelina cried miserably. "I'm never going to dance again!"

Through her tears, Angelina glanced at a framed picture on her bedside table. It was a photograph of her standing beside Miss Lilly, with all the other dancers gathered around them.

"How could you leave us, Miss Lilly?" Angelina sniffled as she picked up the photograph. "We're good dancers, too!"

Angelina gazed at the picture thoughtfully. Suddenly, she had another idea—an idea that would surely convince Miss Lilly to stay!

Early the next morning, Miss Lilly arrived at the train station. She hurried along the platform with the station porter close behind, lugging her heavy suitcases.

The train chugged into the station and squealed to a stop. As the noise and smoke cleared, Miss Lilly was greeted by another sound—music!

She turned around and gasped. Three ballerinas were dancing beside an old record player. Priscilla, Penelope, and Alice were dressed in their tutus and performing perfect pirouettes.

Miss Lilly clasped her hands together in delight.

As the music swelled, William joined the other dancers. He glided toward Miss Lilly and gracefully bowed before her.

Finally, Angelina leaped across the platform. She danced her heart out, knowing this was her last chance to convince Miss Lilly to stay. William rose to meet Angelina, and they twirled round and round as the music slowly faded.

"Beautiful . . . so beautiful, my mouselings," Miss Lilly murmured. "You're all magnificent!"

As the train blew its whistle, Miss Lilly sighed. "Thank you for such a lovely send-off," she said to the mouselings. Then she bent down to gather her luggage.

"But Miss Lilly!" cried Angelina, tears rolling down her cheeks. "We worked so hard. How can you leave us?"

Miss Lilly said tenderly, "Oh, Angelina, it's only for a short weekend."

Angelina blinked. "Weekend?" she asked, her voice quivering. Then she turned to her friends and said again, more joyfully, "Only for the weekend!"

"Oh, Miss Lilly!" Angelina cried with relief as she threw herself into her teacher's arms. The other mouselings gathered around, too, for an enormous hug before Miss Lilly boarded the train.